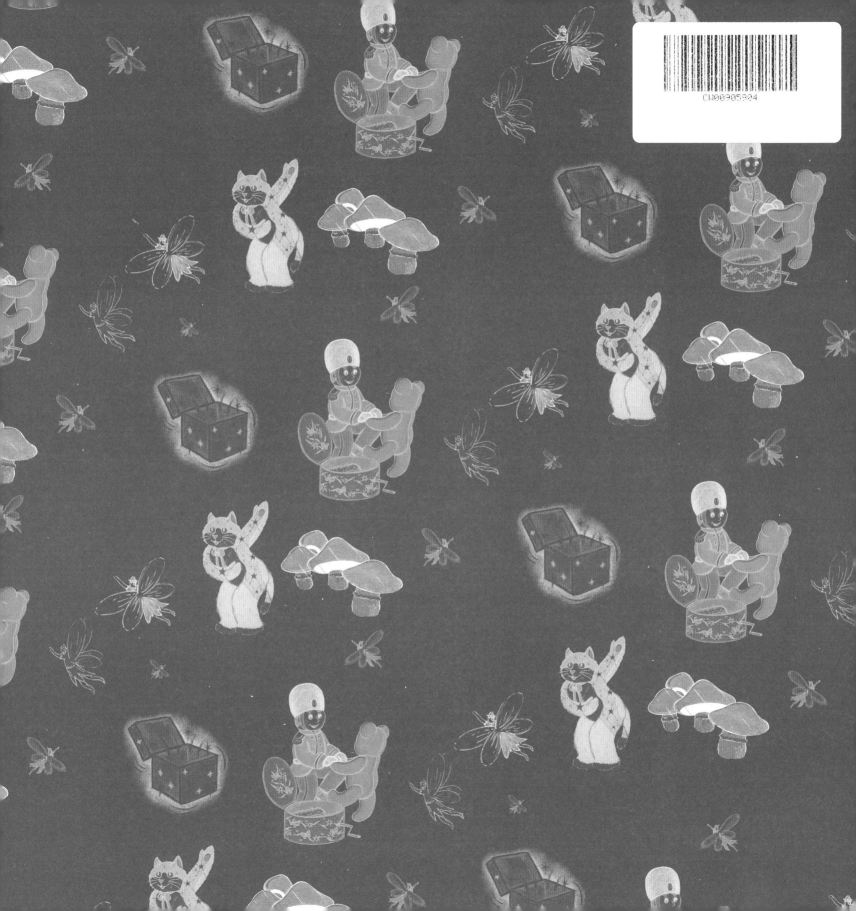

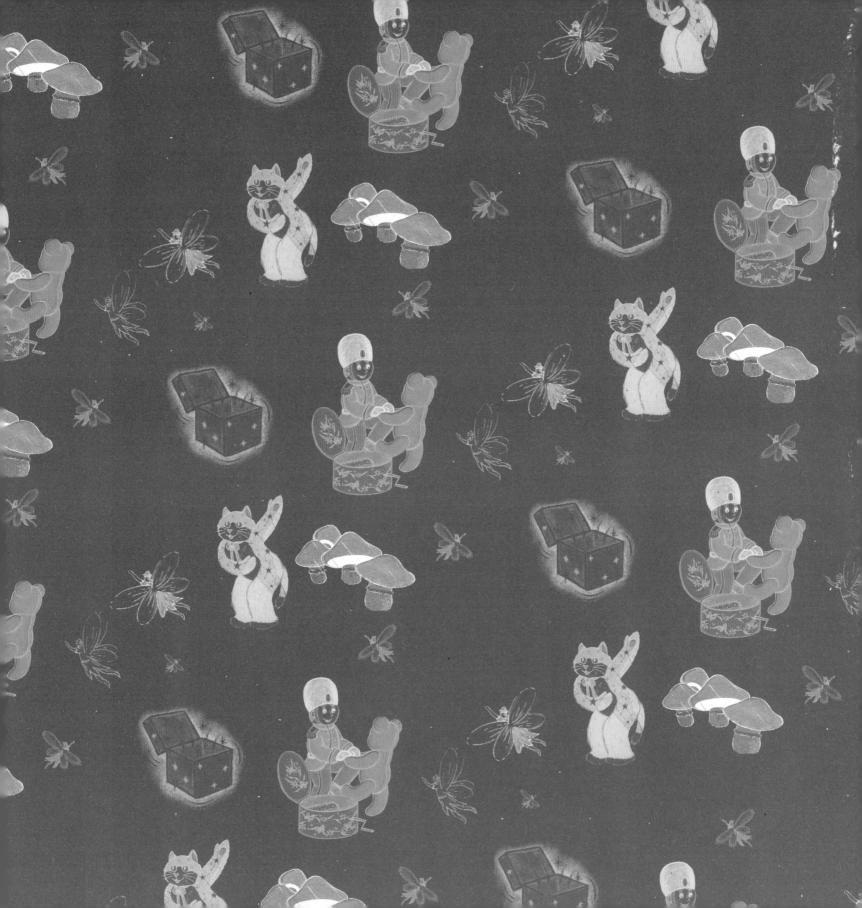

The Birds and the Bun

&

Muzzling the Cat

Published in 2004 by Mercury Books London
20 Bloomsbury Street, London WC1B 3JH

© text copyright Enid Blyton Limited
© copyright original illustrations, Hodder and Stoughton Limited
© new illustrations 2004 Mercury Books London

Designed and produced for Mercury Books
by Open Door Limited, Langham, Rutland

Title: The Birds and the Bun & Muzzling the Cat
ISBN: 1 904668 32 1

The Birds and the Bun

&

Muzzling the Cat

MERCURY BOOKS
LONDON

The Birds and the Bun

There was once a baker's boy who went down Leafy Lane with a basket of bread and buns. As he went he sang a song and swung his basket, and out dropped a bag with a large currant bun inside. The boy did not see the bun falling and he went on his way.

The bun lay in the lane in its paper bag, and as no one came by that way it stayed there for a whole hour.

Then a robin came by and saw it.
"A paper bag, a paper bag!" he cried.

A brown sparrow flew down and pecked at the bag. "There's something inside!" he chirrupped.

Down flew a fine chaffinch and pecked open the bag. "I have pecked a hole!" he sang, "I have pecked a hole!"

Then a big blackbird fluttered down and put his head inside the hole.

"There is a bun inside!" he sang. "A bun, a big currant bun!"

A thrush joined the little crowd and he pecked at the bun. "It is good!" he said. "I shall eat it. It is mine."

"Yours!" cried the robin, indignantly. "What do you mean? I saw the paper bag first!"

"But I told you there was something inside the bag!" chirrupped the sparrow, at once. "I did, I did!"

The chaffinch pushed against the thrush. "Go away!" He cried. "This is my bun. It was I who pecked a hole in the bag."

"But I peeped inside it!" said the blackbird. "The bun is mine. Go away, everybody!"

"You are foolish!" said the thrush, scornfully. "I pecked the bun first – so it is mine. I am now going to eat it!"

Then there was such a noise of quarrelling and chirrupping and singing that no one could hear himself speak. Suddenly there was a large caw and down flew a large black rook.

"What is the matter?" he said, in his deep voice.

Then everyone told him about the bun in the paper bag.

"And each of us thinks it is his," said the thrush. "How can we settle it?"

"I will settle it for you," said the rook. "Now, you all have good voices, I will hear you sing for this bun, and I will give it to the one who sings the best."

"That is a good idea," cried everyone, for they all thought they had fine voices, even the shrill sparrows.

"Very well," said the rook. "Now please turn round so that you have your backs to me. When I say 'Go!' open your beaks and sing loudly for all you are worth, till I say stop."

So the robin, the sparrow, the chaffinch, the thrush and the blackbird all turned round with their backs to the rook, opened their beaks, and waited for him to say "Go!"

"Go!" he shouted. And then you should have heard the robin's creamy trill, the sparrow's loud chirrup, the chaffinch's pretty rattle of a song, the thrush's lovely notes and the blackbird's fluting. Really, it was fine to hear.

They went on and on and on –
and they didn't hear the rook
tearing open the paper bag.

They didn't hear him taking out the bun.
They didn't hear him spreading his great
black wings and flying off into the next field.
No, they went on and on singing, each trying
to outsing the rest.

When they were quite tired of singing, they
wondered why the rook did not tell them to
stop. So the robin looked round

– and he saw that the rook was gone!

He hopped over to the paper bag – and it was empty!

"See, see!" he cried. "The bun is gone – and so is the rook! He has tricked us! Oh, the rascal! Oh, the scamp! Now we have lost our bun!"

"And there was plenty there for all of us!" chirrupped the sparrow, in dismay. "Why did we make such a fuss? We could each have had some – and now we have none!"

They flew off in a rage – and you may be sure the rook didn't show himself for a day or two! And when he did, and happened to meet the others, he cawed politely, and said: "Really, my friends, you have REMARKABLY fine singing voices! Do let me hear you some other time!"

And you should hear them shout at him then!

Muzzling the Cat

Once upon a time there lived a big grey cat with orange eyes. He was called Smoky because his fur was the colour of grey smoke. He used to lie on the sunny wall and watch the birds flying about in the trees.

The birds hated Smoky because he was so clever at catching them. He caught their young ones, too, and that made them very miserable. "Let's have a meeting about Smoky," said the thrushes and blackbirds.

"Perhaps we can think of some way of stopping his dreadful deeds."

So they called a
meeting. The robin
came, full of woe
because one of his
youngsters had

been caught by Smoky the day before.
The wren came, cocking up his perky little
tail. The chaffinch came with his pretty
salmon-pink breast, and the
starling, flashing blue and green
in the sunshine. The sparrow was
there, too, cheeky as usual, as
talkative as the starling.

"Friends," said the big blackbird, opening his beautiful orange beak, "we have met here to-day to talk about that horrid cat, Smoky."

At once there was a great deal of twittering and chattering.

"Silence," said the speckled thrush, lifting up one of his feet. Everyone was quiet.

"Smoky catches us and our young ones in a very cruel way," went on the blackbird.

Muzzling the Cat

29

"We must stop him. How shall we do this? Has anyone any good ideas?"

"Let's all fly round and peck him hard," said the robin, fiercely.

"Well – that would only make him angrier still the next day," said the blackbird. "He would probably kill us all!"

"Let's upset his dish of milk each morning!" cried the wren.

"That's no good!" said the blackbird. "He would be so hungry that he would catch us all the more!"

There was silence for a moment – and then the sparrow and the starling both spoke at once. "Let's-let's-let's..." Then they stopped and glared at one another. They opened their beaks once more. "Let's... let's..."

The starling pecked the sparrow. "Will you be quiet and let me speak?" he shouted.

The sparrow pecked at the starling. "You let me speak!" he answered back sharply.

"Order, order!" said the thrush sharply. "No quarrelling here!"

"My idea is very good," said the starling hurriedly. "Why not MUZZLE the cat?"

"That was my idea, too!" cried the sparrow in a rage. "I was going to say EXACTLY the same thing!"

"You see," said the starling, taking no notice of the sparrow, "if the cat wears a muzzle, it cannot eat us! There is an old dog's muzzle hanging in the garden shed. We could get that and muzzle the cat well with it."

"A splendid idea," said the blackbird. "Yes, the cat shall be muzzled."

"I thought of it first!" chirrupped the sparrow angrily, trying to peck a feather from the starling's wing.

"You're a story-teller!" squawked the starling. "It was my idea!"

"Who is going to do the muzzling?" asked the thrush.

Nobody answered. Nobody wanted that little piece of work.

"Come, come," said the blackbird, "somebody must do it."

"Well, I think it ought to be the one who thought of the idea first," said the thrush firmly.

The starling nearly fell off the tree with fright. The sparrow hid his head under his wing, hoping that nobody would notice he was still there.

"Er... er..." said the starling, at last.

"Well... as the sparrow kept saying just now – it was really his idea, not mine. I ought not to have spoken."

The sparrow took his head from beneath his wing in a temper.

"Ho!" he said, "You say it was my idea, now you think you've got to muzzle the cat yourself! Well... you can have the idea! I don't want it! You said it was yours, and so it is!"

"No quarrelling here!" said the blackbird.
"Both of you shall do the muzzling together!
Sparrow, go and fetch the muzzle from
the garden shed."

Off flew the sparrow,
and came back
with the little wire
muzzle in his beak.
His smart little mind
had thought of an
idea to trick the
starling.

"Come on, starling!" he cried. "It's no use putting it off. It's got to be done. I'm not a coward, if you are!"

The starling shivered with fright.

"Look," said the sparrow, "I've got the muzzle ready – but I can't muzzle the cat by myself, starling. You must go and hold him still whilst I put it on. Come on!"

The starling gave a great splutter of fright. Hold that cat still! Oooooh! The very thought made the starling feel quite faint.

"Do hurry up!" chirrupped the sparrow. "Smoky is lying on the wall. Just fly down and hold him tightly by the neck. Then, as soon as he is quite still, I will slip the muzzle over his mouth."

"Yes, hurry and help the sparrow!" cried all the other birds to the frightened starling.

But he didn't dare to. He spread his wings and flew squawking and spluttering away, leaving the sparrow and the muzzle behind him.

"Coward! Coward!" cried all the birds.

The sparrow was delighted. "Come along, somebody," he cried. "I don't mind who holds the cat still for me. Will you, blackbird?"

"I've got to go back to see my wife," said the blackbird, in a hurry, and he flew off. And before very long the sparrow was left quite alone, chuckling and chirrupping to himself in delight.

Then he heard a voice from below him that made him tremble with fear.

"Ho, little sparrow, I heard all that has been said," said Smoky the cat, with a laugh. "How cowardly all the birds are except you, aren't they? Well, you shall show them how brave you are! I promise to keep quite still, and you shall try to muzzle me.

So come down and do what you want to!"

But alas! The sparrow had fled! The muzzle had dropped down to the ground, and Smoky yawned widely showing his sharp white teeth.

"A fuss about nothing!" he said. "They are all as cowardly as each other.

I shall go and get my bread and milk."

Have you ever heard the starlings talking loudly to one another, or the sparrows twittering in a crowd among the trees?
You'll know what they are talking about now...
how the cat was NEARLY muzzled – but not quite!